ALIEN DUDE!

and

the Attack of Wormzilla!!

Written by E. K. Smith
Illustrated by Peter Grosshauser

Zip Line Publishing

FOR LAKE-
Thanks for the tips.

Published by Zip Line Publishing
P.O. Box 78134
Charlotte, NC 28271

ISBN: 978-0-9883792-0-6

Printed in the United States of America

First Edition

CONTENTS

CooL!

Yuck!

Meet Alien Dude.

He can fly.

He can **MORPH**.

He can do **many**. . .

many. . . .

. . . .many things.

He is Alien Dude!

Chapter 1
WORMS!

"Oh no!" Alien Dude saw worms at school.

"Worms are on my desk!" said the teacher.

"Yuck! Worms are in my shoes!" said a girl.

"Yuck! Worms are in my book!" said a boy.

SLAM!

Alien Dude got up to look around.

"Yuck!" said a boy in the bathroom.
"Worms are in the sink!"

"Yuck!" said a teacher in the hall.
"Worms are in my hair!"

15

"Yuck!" said a girl at lunch.
"Worms are in my hotdog!"

"Who did this?" asked Alien Dude.

Then he went to find out.

Chapter 2
WORMZILLA AND THE HOOK

"Look!" said Alien Dude.

"Go, my **MINIONS**, go!"
said Wormzilla.

22

"I must **stop** Wormzilla and his **MINIONS!**"

23

Alien Dude got an **idea**.

He went up in a tree.

25

Then he **MORPHED** into a hook.

Alien Dude **hooked** Wormzilla.

27

Alien Dude put Wormzilla in the lake.

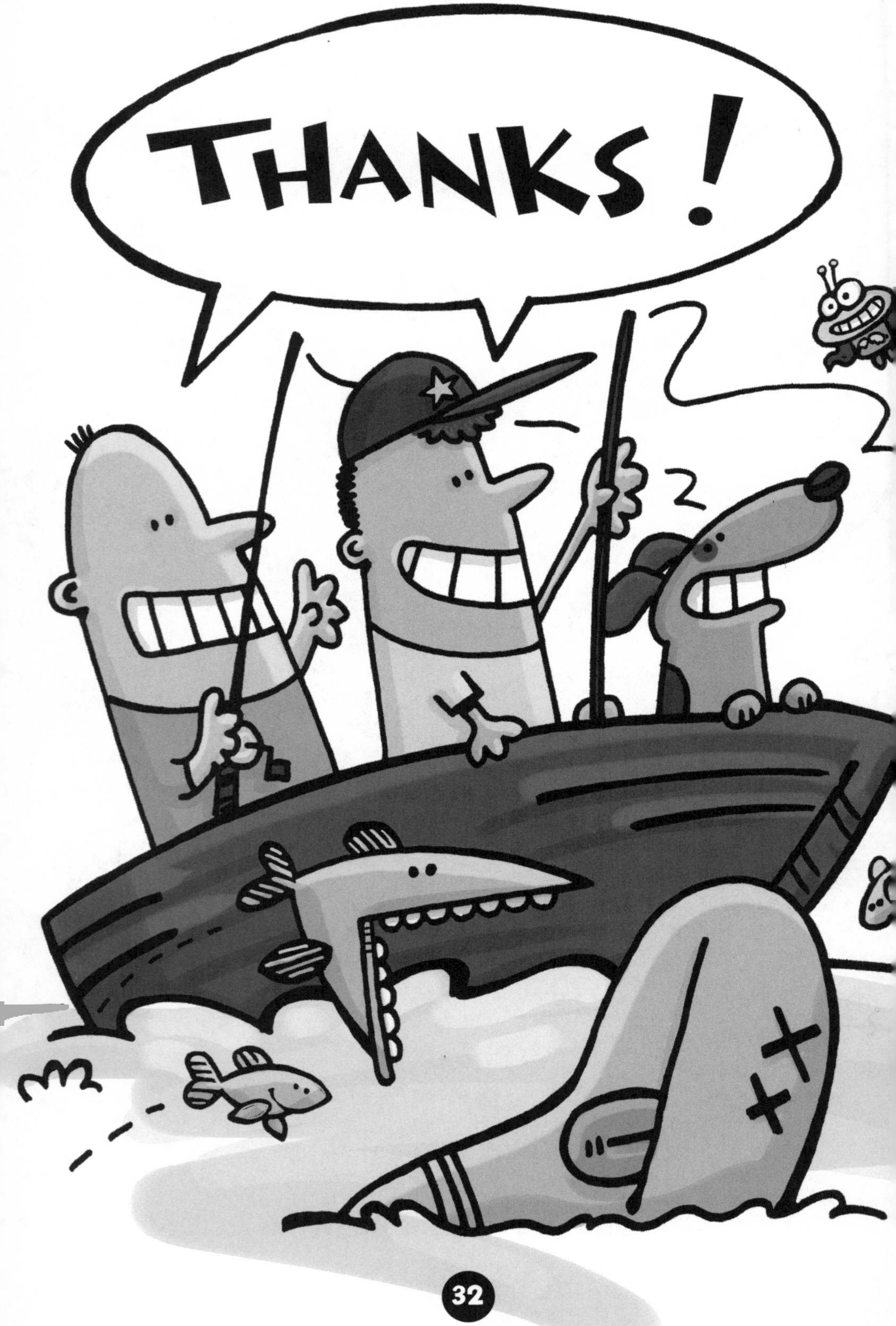
THANKS!

Chapter 3

THE BIRDS

"Get rid of the **worms!**" said the kids.

Alien Dude got an **idea**.

He **FARTED**.

The worms **loved** it!

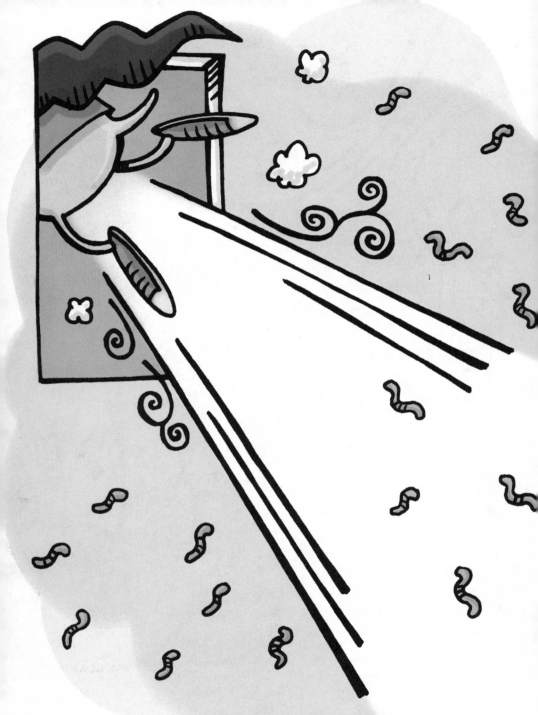

Alien Dude farted and went outside.

The worms went outside with him.

Then Alien Dude sang to the birds.

The birds loved it!

Then they saw the
WORMS.

The birds ate...

and ate...

and ate.

Then a boy said, "Look at the birds!"

"They are too **fat**," he said.

"They are too **fat** to eat more worms!"

Chapter 4
EXPLOSIONS AT THE DUMP

"Now what?" asked a girl.

Alien Dude got an **idea**.

He **FARTED**.

The worms **loved** it!

Alien Dude went to the dump, and the worms went with him.

The worms ate...
and ate...
53 and ate...

and ate and ate and ate until...

Alien Dude went back to school with
WORM GUTS on his face.

"Thank you, Alien Dude!"
said the kids.

Alien Dude
was a hero.

Some Alien Dude **FACTOIDS**:

- Alien Dude can **FART** any time he feels like it.

- Alien Dude wants to have a **MUSTACHE** when he gets older.

- Zip lining is Alien Dude's favorite **SPORT**.

This book is brought to you by your friends at **Zip Line** Publishing

This book is for **BOYS**.

You think **GIRLS** won't read it?